OLiVia'S Secret Scribbles

Music Makers

For Iris and Eva, and marvellous music makers
everywhere!—M.C.

For Maggie, Roxy, Marly and Ellie—D.M.

Scholastic Australia
An imprint of Scholastic Australia Pty Limited
PO Box 579 Gosford NSW 2250
ABN 11 000 614 577
www.scholastic.com.au

Part of the Scholastic Group
Sydney · Auckland · New York · Toronto · London · Mexico City
· New Delhi · Hong Kong · Buenos Aires · Puerto Rico

Published by Scholastic Australia in 2019.
Text copyright © Meredith Costain, 2019.
Illustrations copyright © Danielle McDonald, 2019.

 A catalogue record for this
book is available from the
NATIONAL LIBRARY OF AUSTRALIA National Library of Australia

ISBN: 978 1 76066 004 8

Typeset in KG First Time in Forever, Berrylicious and Sweet Lollipop.

Printed by Hang Tai.

Scholastic Australia's policy, in association with Hang Tai, is to use papers that are renewable
and made efficiently from wood grown in responsibly managed forests, so as to minimise its
environmental footprint.

10 9 8 7 6 5 4 3 2 1   19 20 21 22 23 / 1

Musical Monday

This morning something very special happened in assembly . . .

The Music Makers came to school! They climbed up onto the stage with lots of different musical instruments. And then they made amazing music, just for us!

They played quiet, silvery music

and bright, tootly music

and music like crashing thunder

and music that made you want to get up
and dance!

After assembly finished, the Music Makers visited some of the classrooms. And ours was one of them!

Here are some of the instruments they brought with them.

Things with strings

Double Bass

Violin

Things made out of metal

Trumpet

Trombone

Things you can tap or bang with sticks or your hands

Bongos

Xylophone

African drums

Everyone loved the Music Makers. So we asked Mr Platt if they could come back again tomorrow. But he said they'd be too busy, visiting kids in other schools. ☹ And then he asked us to get out our spelling books because he had some *really* important words he wanted us to learn how to spell.

MR Platt

neck
pack
pick
rock
rocket

I wrote down all the words in my spelling book. But I couldn't stop thinking about silvery harps. And tootling trumpets. And crashing drums.

And neither could anyone else. 🙁

Suddenly, Bethany's arm rocketed into the air. 'Excuse me, Mr Platt!' she said. 'Can we make our own music show? Like the Music Makers did?'

'And play it at assembly?' said Mim.

And then everyone else joined in.

Ple-e-e-ase, MR PLATT!

THat WOULD Be Awesome!

Can I play the HARP?

CaN I play tHe TRUMPET?

But Mr Platt said we couldn't play harps, or trumpets, or drums, or *any* of the instruments the Music Makers played. That's because we didn't have any of those things in our school.

Everyone looked sad.

Then Mr Platt told us all to cheer up, because he'd had a super-amazing idea: we could all play our recorders instead. There's a big box of recorders at the back of the classroom. And we have recorder lessons every Tuesday afternoon.

Everyone looked a bit like this:

Recorders are OK. But they're a bit boring to play. And they all sound exactly the same. Unless someone does a big squeak. Hehehe.

Daisy wrinkled up her nose.
And so did Nico and Samira
and Matilda and everyone
else in our class.

And then I had a super-
amazing idea too, just as the bell went for
the end of school. So I had to keep it to
myself instead of telling Mr Platt. ☹

But I told Matilda all about it on the way
home from school.

Matilda is my best friend. We've been best friends ever since her family came to live in the house behind ours. We do everything together. And we always tell each other all our secret plans.

ME

BFF
MatiLDa

As soon as I got home I grabbed a snack and ran upstairs to my bedroom. Then I sat down at my writing table and scribbled lots of ideas in my special planning book. It took me a few goes before I finally came up with the perfect plan.

Donkey helped.

I can't wait for school tomorrow so I can tell everyone all about it!

☺livia

New Plan Tuesday

I showed Mr Platt my plan as soon as we'd finished our weekly spelling test.

Olivia
neck ✓
pack ✓
pick ✓
rock ✓
rocket ✓
flick ✓
knock ✓
brick ✓
stick ✓
backpack ✓

10/10

Wow!

And guess what? He really liked it! He even asked me to read it out loud to our class.

Here's what I wrote.

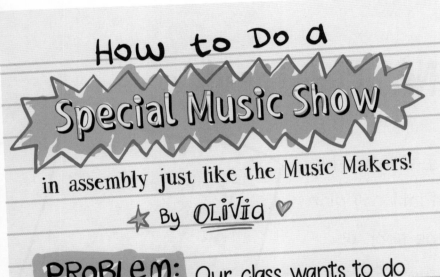

How to Do a
Special Music Show
in assembly just like the Music Makers!

★ By OLIVIA ♡

PROBLEM: Our class wants to do a special music show in assembly. But we don't have any interesting musical instruments to play in it.

SOLUTION:

STEP ①
Look in books for ideas about how to make our own musical instruments. Or invent some new ones all by ourselves!

Blow here →

UP and DOWN

SPIN

TURN

BANG!

STEP ② Make the musical instruments in our classroom.

STEP ③ Have lots of fun playing them at assembly.

STEP ④

Take lots of bows when everyone claps and cheers us!

Everyone loved my plan!

And Mr Platt said we can start making our musical instruments tomorrow! And he is going to ask Mr Martini (our school principal) about us playing in assembly.

Bethany and Mim are really happy about that! And so is everyone else.

I have to go now. Mum is calling me for dinner.

And Donkey is miaowing A LOT. I think he wants to go outside.

I'll write more soon!

☺livia

After dinner . . .

I told everyone our exciting news at dinner.

Me: Some special people came to our school yesterday and played music at assembly. And now *we're* going to be playing music at assembly too.

Mum: Who's we?

Me: Matilda. And me. And Bethany and Mim. It was their idea. And also Ava and Daisy and Sage and Samira and Harry and Nico and EVERYONE in our whole class.

Dad: Sounds like fun!

Me: I know. And we're going to be making

ALL the instruments ourselves. And that part was my idea.

Ella: Our class already did that. Way back when I was in Grade One. It will just be baby stuff. For babies.

Me: Will not.

Ella: Will too.

But it won't. No way. We are going to be making the best musical instruments ever.

Starting tomorrow!

☺livia

Bizz Buzz Wednesday

Mr Platt had some more super–amazing news for us this morning.

Mr Martini said we can play our music show at assembly.

YES!

But guess what?

He wants it to be at the assembly on the last day of term. And school term finishes

next week. Which means we only have six days to get everything ready for it.

OOPS! We'd better hurry up!

Mr Platt took us all to the library to get ideas for things we could make.

As soon as we arrived, Ava and Daisy and Harry and Nico ran straight over to the computer.

Matilda and I went over to see the librarian, Mr Snarski, instead. Mr Snarski knows lots about everything. He always knows exactly which book you are going to need for a project.

SPACE

CHICKENS

DINOSAURS

ROBOTS

MR SnaRski

These are the books he found for us in the library. They are going to be perfect for our project!

We showed the books to Mr Platt. He said we should start with some of the easy-peasy things, like shakers . . .

or cymbals . . .

or kazoos.

Paper towel or
toilet paper tube

Holes

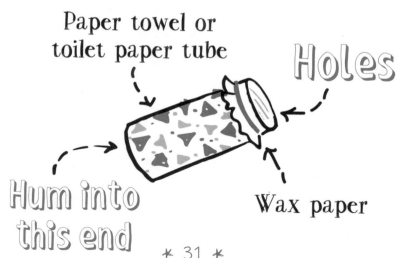

Hum into
this end

Wax paper

My family play kazoos all the time.

Especially when it's someone's birthday.

They make **really** funny sounds. ☺

Everyone else thought kazoos would be fun

to make too. So we started with those first.

Sage and Samira went off to the art
room and came back with a big bag full of
cardboard tubes.

We decorated our tubes with paint and
stickers.

Then we punched little
holes in them . . .

and put squares of wax
paper over the top.

Everyone ran around the
room, playing their kazoos.

Ava's and Daisy's kazoos sounded like
buzzing mosquitoes.

Sage's and Samira's sounded like ambulance sirens.

But Harry's and Nico's sounded like sick cows. Even Mr Platt said so.

After we'd finished playing our kazoos we lined them up on the bench at the back of our classroom. They looked amazing all together. Just like a big, noisy family. ☺

We're going to make cymbals and drums and shakers tomorrow. Mr Platt gave us a list of things to bring to school.

- Coffee cans
- TINS
- OLD CDS
- PLaSTIC BOTTLeS

I want to make them all!

☺livia

Shake It Up Thursday

Something very strange is going on in our classroom. Some of the kazoos from our kazoo family were on the floor when we came in this morning. And others were lying sideways on the bench.

And Harry's and Ava's were missing altogether! They looked everywhere for them. But they couldn't find them. Mr Platt asked if any of us knew anything about it. But nobody did.

Hmmm. It's a MYSTERY!

After roll call, Mr Platt divided up our class into groups, with a captain for each one. I was hoping Mr Platt would ask me to be captain of our group. Being captain is fun!

But he asked these people instead.

Sage   AVa   Harry   Jonno

Jonno's group made the cymbals. They were easy-peasy. So they made some drums out of old coffee cans as well.

LiDS

THICK paper

coffee cans

DRUMS

They weren't very loud though. Not like real drums and cymbals.

Sage's group made shakers out of plastic cups and rice. They dyed the rice rainbow colours and mixed in some sparkly sequins!

Samira taped ribbons to the top of her shaker. They flapped around every time she shook them.

Samira

SHaKER

RIBBONS

Ava's group made maracas.

Mr Platt helped them to blow up balloons and tie knots in the ends. But the balloons

kept trying to escape! They flew all around
the room. ☺

Ava and Daisy made a big bowl of sticky paste out of flour and water. Everyone dipped their hands in the paste and smeared it all over their balloons.

And also all over each other. ☺

They stuck little squares of newspaper on top of the paste. Then they left their maracas on the bench to dry overnight.

Our group made shakers out of plastic drink bottles and beans and toilet rolls for handles.

It was really hard to get the beans into the bottles. They kept spilling down the sides.

So I invented a special Bean-pourer
Innerer.

Here are my plans for it.

Olivia's Super-duper Bean-pourer Innerer!

Beans GO in HERE

ROLLED UP PAPER

TAPE

Beans come OUT HERE

How to Use It

My Bean-pourer Innerer worked really well!

We made handles for our shakers out of toilet paper rolls and decorated them.

They sound really cool when we shake them.

I can't wait until tomorrow when everything is finished and we can play all our instruments together. It's going to be AMAZING!

Olivia

Finish-Up Friday

This morning when we came into our classroom there was more mess. There were little piles of rice and beans all over the bench and on the floor. And also ribbons!

And someone had poked holes in the maracas!

Everyone was talking about who might have done it. Here are Matilda's and my top ideas.

The kids from Mrs Corben's class across the hall. Maybe they are annoyed that

we're playing a music show in assembly,
and they're not.

Ella and her BFF Zoe. Ella did say it was a
project for babies. So maybe she tried to
ruin it. Would Ella do that?

A big rat living under the bench. Rats LOVE
rice and beans.

(YUK! I hope it's not this.)

I'm going to invent a trap to help me find out who it is!

Ava and Daisy stuck tape across their maraca shells to cover up the holes. Then they filled them up with rice and pumpkin seeds, added some handles, and painted them with cool patterns.

COOL PATTERNS

TAPE

PENCIL HANDLES

After lunch, Mr Platt asked us all to choose one of the instruments we'd made.

KAZOO

SHAKERS

coffee CAN DRUM

Then we all lined up across the front of the room and played different songs. We started with *Old MacDonald Had a Farm.* The kazoo players tried to make the sounds of the different animals.

But they all sounded like sick cows. ☹

MWERRR! MWERRR! MWERRR! MWERRRee!

So then we tried *If You're Happy and You Know It.*

But the shakers all made the same shaky sound. And Erik and Remy kept clanging their cymbals in the wrong place. And the kazoos *still* sounded like sick cows!

Mr Platt said he couldn't even tell what song we were playing. ☹

Everything is a great big disaster. And there are only six days to go before our assembly.

And we *still* don't know who's making the mess in our classroom. 😦😦😦

☺livia

Later that night . . .

Donkey and I have been doing some more plans in my planning book.

We're working on ideas
for my trap. ☺

And we're also trying
to think up some new
instruments for our
music show.

I don't think cats are very good at musical stuff. 😞

Maybe Matilda has some good ideas? Or Bethany? Or Mim?

I'm going to ask them all to come over here first thing in the morning.

Olivia

Stormy Saturday

Mim was playing netball this morning so she couldn't come. But Matilda and Bethany came over straight after breakfast. We sat in the hammock in my backyard, flipping through our library books.

Ella came out into the backyard and stood in front of us.

Ella: You all have to come inside. RIGHT NOW!

Me: Who says?

Ella: Mum says. And also me.

I poked my tongue out at her.

Me: You can't make me.

Ella poked her tongue out back at me.

Ella: You're going to get in BIG TROUBLE.

Me: No, I'm not. I'm not doing anything wrong. I'm having heaps of fun RIGHT HERE. And so are Matilda and Bethany.

Matilda and Bethany (together): Yeah.

Me: And also Donkey. And Bob. They're having heaps of fun too.

Ella: Fine. Stay out here then.

Me: Fine. We will.

We waited until Ella had gone back inside.
Then we opened up our library books again.

I saw guitars made out of tissue boxes and rubber bands. And tambourines made out of paper plates and jingly bells.

They all looked like fun to make. And also fun to play! But they weren't special enough to play at our assembly.

What about this one? It's called a Rain stick.

Nah.

It Looks a BIT BORING.

And then guess what happened when
Bethany shook the book?

There was a big BANG-CRASH of
thunder!

And golden lightning zigzagged across the sky!

Donkey jumped out of our hammock and bolted over the fence.

And Bob ran over to his kennel and hid inside it, right at the back.

And guess what happened after that?

It started raining! Soft little ploppy sounds to start off with. Then big, heavy, crashy, splashy raindrops. All over Matilda and Bethany and me and our hammock! We grabbed all the library books and raced inside with them.

Then we ran back outside again and danced around in the garden in the rain.

Until Mum told us to come inside. ☹

Wow. Shaking the picture of that rain stick must have made it rain. And also brought all that crashing thunder!

Imagine what would happen if we had a **real** rain stick!

☺livia

Saturday night

I've been writing a new secret plan in my special planning book.

My secret plan is going to be awesome! Everyone is going to love it, for sure.

But I can't tell you what it is yet. It's a secret. ☺

☺livia

Rain Stick Sunday

Matilda and Bethany and I spent all afternoon up in my bedroom. I put a big sign on the outside of my door.

ALL BIG SISTERS HaVe To KEEP OUT THiS meaNs YOU ELLA!!

The first thing we did was make a rain stick, just like the one in the library book.

Bethany scrunched up a super long piece of foil into a snake shape. Then she added some twists and turns to it.

Then Matilda carefully pushed the foil into a loooooong cardboard posting tube, and sealed off the end.

I carefully tipped handfuls of rice and popping corn into the top of the posting tube. Then we sealed that end off as well, and painted stormy patterns all over the outside.

Matilda wanted to try out our rainmaker straight away! But I wouldn't let her. I didn't want any noisy thunderstorms happening in my bedroom. ☺

I whispered my secret plan I've been working on to her and Bethany instead. Now it's *our* secret plan!

We all sneaked downstairs to the kitchen while super–snoop Ella and the rest of my family were in the lounge room, playing a board game.

Then we started raiding the cupboards, looking for stuff for the next part of our plan.

Hehehe. It's going to be amazing!

😊livia

Music Wall Monday

Bethany and Matilda and I told our class
the secret plan for our music show first
thing Monday morning.

SUPER-DUPER SPECIAL PLAN FOR OUR

CLASS MUSIC SHOW

By OLIVIA, MATILDA and BETHANY

MAIN IDEA Use different musical instruments to tell a story. Just like the Music Makers did!

STEP 1 Bethany shakes the rain stick that we made to make a storm come.

STEP 2 Everyone else in our class plays all the shakers and kazoos and cymbals and coffee-can drums we made to make the sounds of the storm.

(Plus also some clangy pots and pans and saucepan lids to make the really loud parts.)

STEP 3 The audience claps and cheers and we all take a bow.

Everyone in our class loved our plan. But then Harry and Nico came up with an **even better idea!**

So now we're going to make a music wall for our show. We're calling it Grade 2P's Super-Duper Loud Music Wall. It's going to be super-cool!

Here are the plans we made for it.

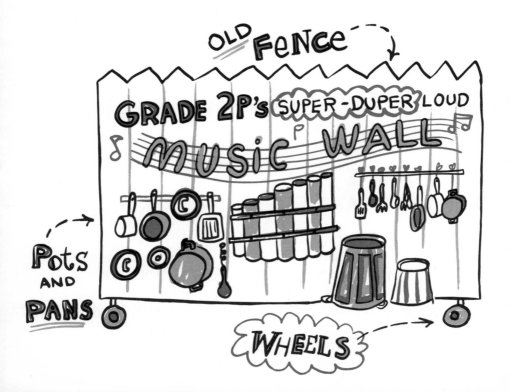

Mr Platt said he had part of an old fence at home that we could use as our wall. And everyone's going to bring in clangy, bangy, tinkly bits for it from home.

I can't wait till Friday so we can all play it together!

☺livia

A bit later . . .

I forgot to show you my invention for catching the person stealing stuff and making all the mess in our classroom!

Here it is.

OLIVIA'S SUPER-DUPER MESS-MAKER CATCHER

How it works:

If the ribbons are gone in the morning, and the pumpkin seeds are all messy, then I know someone is still coming into our room to try to muck up our music show.

I set it all up just before school finished today. I hope it works!

☺livia

FINGERS CROSSED

Bike Wheel Tuesday

I checked the back bench as soon as we came into our classroom this morning.

And guess what? Both of the ribbons were gone! And so were some of the pumpkin seeds!

And then I saw one of the ribbons on the floor, under the window. I wonder how it got there?

Someone has been coming into our classroom again! But who?

Everyone's been bringing in stuff from home for our music wall.

Harry brought in an old bike wheel. Nico's going to spin it around while Harry strokes the spokes with a big spoon. And Daisy found an old fridge rack. She's going to make scratchy storm sounds on it with a wire brush.

BIKE WHEEL

FRIDGE RACK

livia

Wind Chime Wednesday

Our music wall is growing!

Samira brought
in bits of an old
xylophone her little
brother used to play.

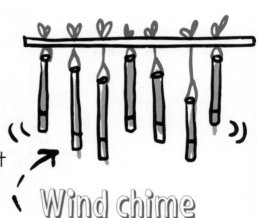

xylophone

And Bethany found
bits from an old,
broken wind chime at
her aunty's place.

Wind chime

And guess what happened after school?

Ella told me she thinks our music show sounds amazing! She showed me how to blow across the top of a bottle to make the sound of the wind in a storm.

I don't think Ella would help me with our music show if she's the one trying to wreck it. So I crossed her and Zoe's names off my list of guesses about who has been breaking our instruments.

WHO IS RUINING OUR INSTRUMENTS?

MRS CORBEN'S GRADE ② CLASS

♥ ~~ELLA~~ ~~AND HER~~ ~~BFF~~ ~~ZOE~~ ♥

A BIG RAT

Hmmm. I wonder if I'm ever going to find out who it is . . .

☹livia

Try It Out Thursday

Our Super—Duper Loud Music Wall is finally finished. We practised our music show all morning.

Mrs Corben's class from across the hall asked if they could come in to our classroom to watch us play. They really liked our show! Everyone clapped and cheered when we finished.

So it can't be them trying to wreck our show either. I crossed their names off the list as well.

~~MRS GORBENS~~
~~GRADE 2 CLASS~~

♡ ~~ELLA AND HER BFF ZOE~~ ♡

A **BIG** RAT

Maybe it *is* a big fat rat after all!

EEK!

How will we ever find out who—or what—
has been coming into our classroom?

Olivia

Showtime Friday

We did our music show today!

Ella always gets a bit nervous before she goes in a show. She says she gets lots of butterflies swirling around in her tummy.

But I had jumping jacks instead. I couldn't wait to get started. ☺

JUMPING JACKS ‑ ‑ ‑→

Mrs Chang, the music teacher, helped Mr Platt wheel our music wall out onto the stage. Then our whole class walked out and stood in front of it.

We waited for everyone to stop talking and pointing. Then Bethany came out to the front of the stage and swished her rain stick from side to side.

Nothing happened.

She swished it again. Louder this time.

Ava's group started shaking their shakers. It sounded like tiny, pattering raindrops.

pitter patter

pitter patter

Sage and Samira picked up their bottles and made soft, shivery, sighing sounds.

WHooo!

WHoo!

Then Harry and Nico and Erik and Remy
joined in behind them, playing their kazoos

louder

and louder

and louder

until the shivery sighs became a huge,
howling wind!

Then everyone else rushed over to the music wall and started banging and clanging and bashing and crashing on it!

It sounded exactly like a big, booming thunderstorm!

Everyone in the hall looked super amazed!

At the end, we all lined up and took a bow.

The audience clapped and cheered us! ☺

It was the best assembly performance
EVER!

And you'll never guess what Matilda and I saw on the way back to our classroom . . .

Cheeky thing!

PHEW! A bird coming into our classroom is heaps better than a rat. ☺

☺livia

Read them all!

OLiVia's Secret Scribbles

 My NEW Best Friend

 My (Almost) Perfect Puppy

 AMAZING Acrobats

 Super Science Stars

 The BIG Chicken Mystery

 Box Car Racers

 Music Makers

More books coming soon!